PRAIS

Top 10 Romance of 2012, 2015, and 2016.

One of our favorite authors.

Buchman has catapulted his way to the top tier of my favorite authors.

A favorite author of mine. I'll read anything that carries his name, no questions asked. Meet your new favorite author!

M.L. Buchman is guaranteed to get me lost in a good story.

I love Buchman's writing. His vivid descriptions bring everything to life in an unforgettable way.

LOVE IN A COPPER LIGHT

A NIGHT STALKERS CSAR ROMANCE

M. L. BUCHMAN

Buchman Bookworks

SIGN UP FOR M. L. BUCHMAN'S NEWSLETTER TODAY

and receive:
Release News
Free Short Stories
a Free Starter Library

Do it today. Do it now.
www.mlbuchman.com/newsletter

Other works by M. L. Buchman:

$\mathcal{T}$he Tonopah Test Range Airport tower gave them clearance and they were gone. Control towers didn't want any return response; they just wanted you out of their airspace. So their helo lifted into the airspace of the Nevada Test and Training Range—the NTTR—and raced away from Tonopah without a word.

"This next part always freaks me out."

"And you say that every time, Copper." Vince Jawolski was flying low and fast, piloting their combat search-and-rescue helicopter toward their hold position for tonight's training exercise.

It was true, she did always say it, but that didn't make Penny "Copper" Penrose feel one bit less freaked. Not that she was worried about the battle—real or simulated—but rather that there was one in progress and their job was to *wait.* CSAR aircraft didn't risk their precious medics until someone actually needed help.

In minutes they were circling five miles and ninety seconds outside the primary battlespace deep in the heart of the NTTR—five thousand square miles of blasted-to-hell desert. It was the perfect place to stretch their Black Hawk's rotor blades a little bit. "Blue Helm" was a massive exercise to keep skills fresh and shake the bugs out of new tactics—without having someone shooting live rounds at them while they were doing it.

Five helos. That was their concern in tonight's training scenario, out of the fifty aircraft and fifteen hundred ground troops spread across the Nevada desert.

The two transport birds had already delivered their 75th Rangers elements, to mess with a tank corps from the 10th Mountain, and slipped away.

Two heavy gun platforms—one DAP Hawk and one Little Bird—were circling high above on overwatch.

And one kick-ass CSAR team all set to pull out any injured when the shit—simulated shit—*did* hit the fan. The six of them had been together for a while and she loved what they could do. But circling out of sight of the battle, there was nothing to see in this ass end of the NTTR except the occasional flight of F-35 jets off to test their mettle in some other section of the exercise. Meanwhile, she was getting tired of having the same night-vision view painted on the inside of her visor as they circled behind a low range of jagged ridges of broken rock.

While she waited for the call, she wondered what David was up to tonight. Was he—

Shit!

She'd been rid of that disaster for two months—splattered across the windscreen like an entire fleet of pulped butterflies—and still her mind went there. Why did she naively keep hoping? Civilian men *never* understood military women. It was like strong women just didn't compute in the civvie world; which sucked for her. Strong women didn't really compute in the military world all that often either. She'd seen too many female soldiers who chose to play the slut role to get attention or the little sister role to avoid it. She wanted to play the herself role—and it wasn't getting her crap.

Penny sat in her copilot's seat and tapped her way across the three status screens she was monitoring in a fast rotation. It wasn't quite a nervous twitch—at least so she liked to assure herself—even if it would look that way to anyone able to see what was flashing across the inside of her helmet's visor.

System status. Engine temperature: stable at 1,950 degrees Fahrenheit. Hydraulic and pressure systems online. Fuel: 87%. Twenty-seven different readings.

Flight status. Two-zero feet AGL—above ground level. Slow cruise: twenty knots. Running dark: infrared lights only. Heart of the NTTR. Nineteen different facts.

Battlespace. Still five miles and ninety seconds away. Two gunship helos at three and five thousand feet, and a drone at thirty thousand. The transport birds had returned to base— they had it easy now that they'd survived landing their teams. Easy unless things went badly and they had to extract the inserted Rangers under heavy fire. But the ground elements were holding strong and reporting no casualties.

The whole situation made for one messy tactical readout with every single identified fighter—good guy or bad— represented on a 3D map of the terrain by a symbology that had taken a months to learn but was now second nature.

System status. Twenty-seven readings…no changes.

Flight status…

Penny had never been able to help herself. She'd flown combat for too many of her years in the service. Every nerve in her body, and most definitely her adrenal glands, *knew* they were supposed to be in the heart of the battle. In the zone. Riding the edge.

Just because this battle was simulated didn't change squat.

Since she'd gone CSAR, now she was off to the side, waiting while others fought. Her body was here, but her body's chemistry was deep in the simulated action.

System status. All nominal.

Flight status...

By flicking through them fast enough, she could actually spot anything that changed in real time across all three spaces. All nominal. As if *that* wasn't enough to make her crazy.

She'd done this so many times, she was able to do it automatically and still harass the team. She was a multi-tasking kind of girl.

And one task was *not* going to be thinking about a jerkwad civilian named David. Distraction. Definitely needed one.

"Calling me Copper, that's another thing!" Penny groused over the intercom to her crewmates. She didn't know why she even tried, it was one battle she was never going to win. With the name of Penelope Penrose and copper-red hair, the "Copper" nickname had been inevitable. "Why you're just as bright as a copper penny!" was a pickup line that she usually answered with mere disdain, unless she'd been drinking, then it might be with her knee—she was tall enough to peg most men easily. Fighting battles is what she did.

Too bad everybody on their flight had learned not to answer her now, even if they didn't change their tune. Not her pilot, not the two crew chiefs perched at their miniguns, and not the two medics along for the ride until they got the call.

"Lame-os!" She teased the lot of them.

It earned her a chuckle from starboard gunner Xavier Jones who sat at a minigun mounted close behind Vince's pilot seat.

Unlike normal CSAR birds that went unarmed into

battle, the Night Stalkers flew fully armed helos—without a Red Cross emblem—that just happened to carry a couple of medics. The Night Stalkers flew to places no one else could go, so they often had their own CSAR support.

"Long as you get me back in time for my wedding, I'll call you anything you want…Copper!"

"You're no help, Jones." He'd hooked up with Noreen Wallace, one of the crew's two medics. And like several other of their crews in the 5th Battalion E Company, command was letting them serve together—unique in the whole military as far as she knew. "How is it that no one ever tagged you with a nickname, Noreen?" Everyone else had one, though other than hers they weren't used all that often.

"No one dares. I'm a freakin' force of nature, that's why. Or so Xavier keeps telling me."

"It's true. Sure won't catch this boy messing with that." The six-four super-soldier Xavier would be the serious, hardcore pillar in any relationship that didn't have Noreen on the other side of it. If Penny was black, shorter, and a medic, she'd want to grow up to *be* Noreen Wallace. As it was, she had three strikes against that dream.

System status.

Flight status.

Battlespace.

It felt as if she had nothing to do, even if that wasn't true. Copilot on a CSAR Black Hawk helicopter was never a dull seat. One of the many things she loved about flying for the US Army's 160th SOAR Night Stalkers.

"What would you like to be called?"

She blinked and lost track of her screens. Barry Goldsmith, Medic Two, never spoke to her directly. He was always pleasant and had a decent sense of humor, but something in her quashed every comment. No one had ever actually asked her that, so she didn't have a quick answer.

"I'm guessing that 'Red' would be too cliché for you," Barry continued over the intercom.

"I might have hospitalized the last dude who tried to call me that—back in tenth grade. He probably could have used your help."

"Okay 'Red' is out. I probably wouldn't have been able to stabilize his condition for transport; remember I was in tenth grade at the same time."

Actually she hadn't known that. Barry was definitely the "mature one" on their crew; which wasn't actually saying much. They were all deeply trained pros, had to be to fly with the Night Stalkers, but that didn't seem to stop their bird being loaded up with a bunch of goofballs at heart—herself included. She kept her silence until she had the rhythm of her flashing screens rolling again.

System status.

Flight status.

Battlespace.

System... God the waiting was killing her. David had always—*shit!*

"I've got to have some worthy trademark besides my name being Penny and my hair color. And no, my ex-boyfriend's consistent focus with the shape of my chest doesn't count."

Ex-boyfriend?

"When did that happen?" Barry clamped his jaw shut, but it had just slipped out of him. He'd totally missed the "ex-" happening, though he *absolutely* remembered them getting together. He'd gone on a bender the night he'd heard about it—then had to report himself unfit for duty when a surprise mission cropped up the next day. He hadn't touched a drink since, not even a beer.

"Couple months back, the misogynistic prick. He couldn't cut the grade. Turns out he thought I was sure to quit during our last tour in the Dustbowl because no woman could possibly hack Afghanistan. He'd also been counting on me washing out—'fired' he called it—because a woman couldn't possibly be good enough to fly big, nasty helicopters."

"What an ass." As if Barry could be so proud of his own actions. His bender had been because he was sick of not being able to speak to the most amazing woman he'd ever met. By the stories she'd told at first, it had sounded like David was the one, which meant he'd lost her. He'd

7

completely missed when her David-stories had fallen out of their helo banter.

Well, if David was dumb enough to mess it up with Penny, Barry wasn't going to fall into the same trap of silence he had before. "Sounds like he didn't deserve you. Too stupid to know what he had."

That had all of the rear-enders—those who flew in the back of the helicopter—twisting around to look at him. Noreen, and the two crew chiefs: Xavier, and Mason "Jar" Buckley.

"What?" he mouthed at them.

He tried not to read too much into Noreen's smile before she turned back to quadruple checking their med supplies —*her* pre-battle habit.

"Thanks, Barry. He *was* an ass. Next time could someone tell me sooner?" Penny answered after a thoughtful silence. "Final fight was him demanding I quit so he'd know I would live long enough to raise our future children."

"You were engaged?" How had he not known any of this about Penny?

"Not even close. He was just that disconnected from reality."

"What did you do?" Women always tongue-tied him, but only the ones he was attracted to. It was a ridiculous curse that thankfully only he knew about. How many stunners had left him an opening in high school, ones who he'd been too awed to speak to, before they'd lost interest and drifted off?

"I did what any Night Stalker woman would do, I dumped his ass. Then I sugared his Porsche 911 Targa's gas tank."

"No way!" Noreen's merry laugh blasted from the intercom.

But it didn't sound like the Penny he knew.

"Way! Well, actually... Turns out that sugar doesn't really do much damage if you dump it into the gas tank, but most people don't know that. So I sprinkled it on the ground by the gas cap, dumped the empty bag on the ground, then sat back in the shadows to watch the fun. Man did it mess with his head. He actually cried—down on his knees hugging his bumper. It was beautiful! More than the bastard ever did over me."

Barry laughed, "You rock it, girl." Now *that* sounded exactly like Penny.

Once again the rear-enders were all looking at him in surprise. He was just glad that Penny was up in her seat facing forward.

*P*enny was still puzzling over Barry's sudden chattiness when she spotted it.

Flight status.

Battlesp—

"Vince!" Her call was all that was necessary.

Vince carved a turn for the heart of the battle before the official call came in. Full up on the collective, Black Hawk's nose down for maximum speed.

"Little Bird down. Little Bird down," sounded over the radio in that perfect flat voice that battle commanders always had. "Sector Alpha. Three. Fiver."—the "-er" making the number clearer over the radios.

On the battlespace display, Penny had seen the tiny attack helicopter stumble in midflight. It was like it had tripped on something hard.

The problem with CSAR holding safely at ninety seconds outside the battlespace was that they *were* ninety seconds outside the battlespace.

The pilot of the Little Bird was doing a hell of a simulation as he tumbled out of the sky. End-os, rolls, rolling back the other way.

Then a truly chilling, "Mayday. Mayday. Mayday." Nobody called that during a training scenario. She'd had to do it once in the Dustbowl when an RPG had eaten her tail rotor, and the words were almost impossible to speak.

No one was shooting live ammo, so something critical had broken. And it had broken bad.

With her nerves amped up, it felt as if, for that ninety seconds, they were slogging through molasses. The meters flew by at the Black Hawk's top speed, but still the seconds crawled by one at a time.

Sixty seconds...

On the tactical display, the Little Bird wasn't going down gracefully, but it wasn't a dead-stick plummet either. Someone was still fighting to save the bird.

"Medics alert," she called over the intercom. "MH-6M attack Little Bird going down. This is not a simulation."

"Any other helpful news for us?" Barry Goldsmith, the handsome golden-hair boy from Brooklyn, was always looking at the bright side of everything. The more intense things got, the quirkier he got. One hell of a defense mechanism—something she'd always appreciated about him. One of many things.

"Sure. Simulated battle is still in full swing," Penny shot for a light tone, but doubted that she succeeded as she watched the horrifying flight playing out on her display. The thousands of personnel, and billions of dollars of aircraft and hardware in motion for this exercise didn't stop due to one falling helicopter. They probably assumed it was a simulated loss. "We're planting you in a hot LZ on the fly."

"Excellent. My panic response was out of practice anyway. Medic Two ready. Noreen?"

"Medic One. Always ready," Noreen sounded even more ramped up than usual for her. Of course she was marrying their totally studly gunner, starboard-side gunner Xavier Jones in a few days.

Forty-five seconds...

Penny had expected the two medics, Noreen and Barry, to get together. They were always so chummy that they even sounded like a couple. She'd done her level best to not be jealous of Noreen for getting him. Then Xavier showed up and kicked Noreen's feet out from under her—or more likely the other way around.

Just watching the two of them had shown her everything that was wrong with David, and she'd dumped his sorry ass.

But Barry still hadn't spoken to her outside of duties, which had been a bummer. Had to be something wrong with her, if a nice guy like him was avoiding her. Or so she'd thought until just now.

Thirty seconds...

The Little Bird gave a final flinch in the air. Fifty feet above the ground, the pilot managed to halt their plummeting descent by some miracle of piloting that was impressive even by Night Stalker standards. It wavered in the air for several seconds, then simply fell straight down.

A cloud of dust obscured it from view.

"We're staying down for this one," Vince announced. It was a dangerous choice. Normally CSAR dumped off the medics, scooted their twenty-million-dollar bird up to safety, then slid back to ground again when they were ready for pickup. On the ground they were vulnerable, even to simulated forces. Every extra second was a risk for the aircraft, but it was also a second less that it would take to transport the victims.

Penny wondered if anyone else even knew about the

emergency other than them. The Mayday had come in on the CSAR frequency—it was standard practice to not disrupt other battle communications.

*C*ontact!

He and Noreen hit the ground running before the CSAR bird had fully settled on its wheels.

Barry was first on site, and wished he wasn't. The MH-6M Little Bird, nicknamed the Killer Egg for all the weapons it carried, was little more than a Plexiglass bubble barely big enough for the pilot and copilot. The tiny backseat had been filled with the big ammunition cans for their side guns. Engine behind, rotor above, two skids and a tail boom: that's all there was to it.

Two things had saved the pilots' lives. The nose had plowed into the blown-loose dirt around a crater made during some previous training, and their ammo cans were empty—light-based scoring weapons had been mounted in place of the heavy guns. If the cans had been full, a quarter-ton of ammunition would have slammed into the backs of their seats and probably crushed them.

Impossibly, the Little Bird was still running. Its rotor blades had been broken off, but the rotor head still spun fiercely to the screaming whine of the damaged turbine.

Not his problem.

Noreen circled to help the copilot.

Barry's trained responses were already doing a triage on the pilot. Max Engel. *Shit!* They had breakfast together this morning over a game of backgammon.

Pulse: fast and light.

Breathing: yes, airway clear.

Eyes: still responsive, though he was out cold.

No obvious breaks. Nearside leg and arm appeared okay. Barry reached over to check Max's other arm where his hand was still holding onto the collective control beside the seat.

Except it wasn't. His hand was, but there was no arm attached below the elbow. A chunk of the shattered windshield had sliced it off during the crash landing. If it had happened aloft, Max would already have bled out.

Someone reached in through the missing front windshield and began tapping controls. In seconds, the pained scream of the dying engine began to ease.

It took Barry three tries to get a grip on what was left of Max's arm. Once he finally had a firm hold on it, he managed to yank free a tourniquet, but couldn't get it looped on through the spray of blood. The person shutting down the helo reached in and helped him place and tighten it. Max would certainly never fly as pilot again. Talk about a lousy deal of the cards; Max loved to fly.

Unable to do more inside the crumpled cockpit, Barry popped the release on the safety harness. It would take two people to get him out, but Noreen was busy with the semiconscious copilot.

"Take his head."

The person tapped three more controls and the helicopter finally fell silent and went dark. All Barry could hear now was the distant *crump* of flashbangs which had taken the place of major explosives. There were light bursts of simulated fire from the helo's two miniguns as Mason and Xavier protected the grounded CSAR bird from "enemy forces."

The person raced around and took careful hold of Max's helmet.

"Keep his neck in the best alignment with his spine that you can."

"I know what to do." Penny. Of course she would be there when needed. He could always count on Penny.

Once they had him prone and Barry had a pair of IVs pumping fluid and blood back into him, Penny turned aside for a moment.

He heard her retching her breakfast out in the dirt, then she was back and helping him with a steady hand.

"*Y*ou did really great."

It didn't feel as if she had. Penny sat in the ER waiting room and stared at the sleeves of her flightsuit, as did most of the other people there. She had washed her hands—scrubbed them hard—but Max's blood had bathed her up to the elbows, and spattered her everywhere else before they'd staunched the flow.

"Penny," Barry's arm came around her shoulders, "you really did. Don't know if I could have saved him by myself."

She shook her head.

"Penny?" Barry was worried.

About her mental state. How in hell was she supposed to explain what was really bothering her?

"Hey, Copper," he made it a tease.

She looked at him.

So close, so kind and worried—she couldn't ignore that.

"It's not the blood that's bothering me. I don't even think it's what happened to Max, though I'm sorry as hell for him. He handled a big part of my training—a damn good man to have at your back."

"Then what is it?"

"Gonna sound stupid."

"Try me."

Penny scraped at a bit of dried blood on the back of one of her fingernails. She'd had friends die before—had worn their blood more than a few times.

"C'mon or I'll start calling you Copper Penny."

"I am..." Penny wanted to look away from his deep blue eyes, "unconscionably glad to be alive. Time is so goddamn precious and I've wasted so much of it. I feel ashamed."

Barry started chuckling. He jostled her with the arm she hadn't noticed he still had around her shoulder.

"What?"

"I *am* sitting next to CSAR pilot Penny Penrose of the 160th SOAR Night Stalkers highly decorated 5th Battalion E Company, right?"

"I know that. That's not what I'm talking about."

Barry squinted his eyes his blue eyes at her. "Then... what's the topic?"

A doc interrupted them. Operation was done, they'd cleaned up the amputation. Max had come out from under the drugs just long enough to show no brain damage from blood loss, but not long enough to know he'd lost both his arm and his career before they'd put him back under. He was stable enough that they were shipping him to the VA hospital near Sacramento so that he'd wake up near his family.

Barry had led her out of the antiseptic hospital and into the clean desert air.

They were out in the cool desert in time to watch the sunrise over the NTTR.

"Why are you talking to me now?"

"What are you so ashamed about wasting time on?" Barry sat outside himself for a moment and wondered how he was actually speaking to Penny Penrose about something other than a mission. But the opportunity was too precious to waste.

As the sunrise progressed, they walked together across the airfield, headed to the SOAR hangar on the Tonopah Airport. Only a mile away, it wasn't worth requisitioning a jeep. There was traffic associated with the on-going training exercise, but theirs had been the only traffic toward the hospital. No one passed to offer them a lift, for which Barry was grateful.

The sun had warmed the sky to a dusky red that matched the color of Penny's lovely hair.

"Give, Copper Penny. Or I'll call you Red next."

"Like living dangerously, do you, Barry?"

Better to answer with a question than the truth. "Talk to me, Penny."

She stopped and stared out at the desert. The horizon was

shifting from red to pink for three-sixty around. He loved the desert sunrises, where the whole sky colored at once so that it seemed the sunrise could come from any direction and surprise you.

This time he gave her the silence to collect her thoughts.

The sun had finally revealed its plan of attack for the day and was a hard yellow glow, not quite cracking over the Kawich Range yet. The light caught in her hair until it shimmered. Her skin was so pale that a brush of freckles across her nose stood out even in this light.

The sun had broken free of the hills and begun its climb into the morning before she finally spoke.

"David is what I'm ashamed of. The men before him. The time I wasted with them. Max almost died last night."

"Is it Max you're interested in?" *Please say no.* That would be awful in so many ways.

"Max? No. He's got a girl in San Francisco. Good one, he says. Hopefully she'll stick when she sees what happened."

Barry had heard the same news, but he'd missed the whole breakup between Penny and David, so he could have missed something with Max as well.

"After last night, I'm just aware that I don't want to waste any more time. I've wanted to be like Noreen Wallace since the moment I met her, but I could never figure out how. Now I know why I wanted to be like her. She's happy. She's honestly and thoroughly happy. On top of that, she's marrying a damn good man and knows it. I want a good man like that. One who makes me smile and feel good about who he is and who I am. Who we are together."

She started walking again, kicking up dust as if to watch it catch the light. Or maybe as if kicking away her past choices. Barry liked the second possibility for himself and he fell in beside her to kick away some of his own dust.

"Now tell me why you've suddenly started talking to me."

"The truth?"

"The truth," Penny nodded emphatically.

"Sure you can handle it?" At the teasing tone, he felt more like himself than he ever had talking to her. Focusing on the upside had always been his goal, and now he truly was.

"I'm sure, Barry," and the quirk of a smile gave him hope. She was a top flier in the best helicopter unit in the world. And the best feature on the beautiful redhead was her smile.

"What the hell," he put his bets all in. This time he was playing to win. "I'm hoping to convince you that I'm that good man."

"*I* know you're a good man. Otherwise—" Then Penny's brain went sideways on her and she stumbled to a halt.

Barry stopped and watched her. At first his eyes were cautious, but soon she could see the humor rising into them. The smile climbing up in close formation.

"What…" but she didn't know what she wanted to ask. "Why…" didn't help either. "But…" she waved her hand helplessly. It might have been toward their CSAR helicopter that they had nearly reached, though now disappearing into the heat shimmer rising off the vast expanse of pavement. Or she might have been waving toward the past.

"Why haven't I said anything before?"

She could only nod.

"Gearing up the nerve to talk to you took a while."

"A damn long while."

"Well, I was almost there, and then you starting seeing David. Seemed like keeping my mouth shut was the right thing to do after that."

"*Almost there?* What stopped you?"

"You're scary as hell, Copper Penny."

"I am? No I'm not. Even if I am, you're a combat medic who just saved Max's life. How can you be afraid to talk to a girl?"

He shrugged uncomfortably, "When it's you. I am."

Penny scrubbed a hand through her thick hair, then began walking slowly toward the parked helo. "Why?"

"Because in addition to being drop dead gorgeous, you're also the most impressive woman I've ever met."

"Me? Maybe the military me. There's a whole me you don't know that's a total mess."

Barry grabbed the shoulder of her flight suit as she reached to open the cargo door. She wanted to see if they'd cleaned it up yet. He turned her away to look at him.

"It's *exactly* the you that *I* know. I've been watching you a long time—on and off the flightline. It's just that I didn't realize until last night that you weren't with David anymore. I wasn't going to miss my opportunity again, even if the answer was no."

"The answer to what?" Penny was feeling all muddle-headed. Maybe it was the heat. Or Max's injury. Or—

"The answer to the question of—will you go out on a date with me?"

"Well, at least you aren't asking me to marry you and have kids."

"Not yet," Barry's smile said he knew exactly what he'd just done to her brain.

"So what's this date going to be?" It was the best defense she could come up with to buy her a moment to think. The screens of her life were changing far too fast for her to focus on. All systems...in flux!

"Well, we're both going to be at Xavier and Noreen's wedding in a couple days, care to be my date?"

"You want our first date to be a *wedding?*"

"Sure." Whatever hesitancy and silence Barry Goldsmith had always shown to her had evaporated with the morning light. "Breaching unknown territory together."

"Let me guess. You're expecting me to be the one who catches the bouquet?"

"I can always hope."

Penny really didn't know what to do with him. He was handsome as all hell, a great guy, and a top medic with the same elite outfit she'd spent years clawing to get into.

And...she liked him. Liked him a lot. She'd seen his work, his dedication, and his kindness under the very worst of circumstances. And she had no real secrets from him either. He'd had every opportunity to see the good and the bad of her over their last year together.

"A date at a wedding with me catching the bouquet," she repeated, but it didn't sound nearly as strange as the first time she'd said it.

"Uh-huh." His happy tone had her considering various ways she could wipe that smile off his face.

But she didn't want to. So, rather than following her normal pre-flight procedures with men, she'd implement a change of protocol.

"What do you say, *Red?*" Now he was just asking for it.

"A date?" She decided that for Barry she just might want to be the woman catching that bouquet. "But we haven't even kissed yet."

"I know how to cure that, Penny from Heaven."

So did she. And if Barry wanted to see her that way, she was going to let him.

Like the good pilot she was, she didn't bother answering with words.

IF YOU ENJOYED THIS, YOU MIGHT
ALSO ENJOY:

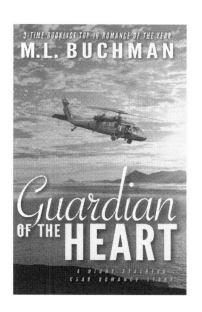

GUARDIAN OF THE HEART
(EXCERPT)

"*D*on't be looking at her, Jones! Are you crazy, man?"

Master Sergeant Mason "The Jar" Buckley (he was kind of short and barrel-chested) yanked hard enough on Xavier's safety harness to almost knock take him down on the hangar's floor. They were buddy-checking their gear before saddling up onto a Black Hawk helicopter headed way out into hell-and-gone ISIS country. Even though the overheads weren't very bright, the darkness of Iraq's Balad Air Base was like a black door across the hangar's maw.

The Jar yanked Xavier's harness the other way. Maybe Mason didn't like his sucky nickname (Xavier had one he hated with a passion and could only hope he'd finally left Stateside). Maybe Mason had it in for new guys to the unit; perhaps he was just trying to make his point.

Another possibility: maybe The Jar was an asshole.

"Why? She yours? Can't hurt a guy to look," Xavier didn't appreciate the manhandling. There was no need to bust his ass *before* he went aloft. Besides, the medic on the other side of the brightly lit hangar—shouldering a pack clearly labeled

"Medical"—was well worth a second look, and a third. She was lightly built, but pulled on forty pounds of gear like it weighed nothing more than feather pillows. She wasn't model material, more the hottest-girl-in-school type—the one so hot that no one ever stood a chance. Thick black hair that fell straight to her shoulders, coffee-and-cream skin, and an attitude like kick-ass sunshine after a long winter.

"Hell no!" Masson looked aghast. "She's not mine. She's not anybody's. That's the Guardian of the Night—the goddamn Angel of Death. You don't want her evil eye on you. Bad luck, brother. Seriously bad luck." Mason picked up the FN-SCAR combat rifle from the table and slammed it against Xavier's chest.

Xavier slipped the strap around his neck and made sure it hung out of the way across his chest.

"Dude's right, you know," one of the pilots, also donning his kit, leaned over. "Something about her is way different." Then he and his copilot jogged toward the darkness.

"You're still lookin'."

"Didn't know they built women like her." Where Xavier came from the women were either jovial mamas with the best kinda curves on the planet (even when they got all out of control they were still mighty good) or they were lean (like anorexic crackhead lean) and mean (big on the mean). This one stood five-eight on a tall day, athlete's curves rather than a plus-size model's, and was joking with another medic as they moved off toward the waiting helo, disappearing into the darkness.

"They don't build women like her anywhere," Mason continued but still wasn't looking where she'd gone. "Nobody's that scary."

"What? The evil eye, Angel of Death crap?" When Xavier was done with crosschecking Mason, he slammed Mason's rifle into his chest just as hard as Mason had into him.

Mason only nodded fiercely. Man looked spooked, which didn't seem right on a master sergeant of the Night Stalkers.

Xavier tapped at each of the pouches on his own vest to make sure nothing was missing: magazines for his sidearm, mags for his rifle, small med kit of his own, spare batteries for his night-vision goggles and radio, the NVGs and radio themselves. He counted items but came up one short.

He did it again, then figured out what he was missing when he slapped his own head. Helmet. Sitting right there on the table. Damn! First day on the job, he seriously wanted to perform, not be some fresh-meat laughing stock. He'd had enough of that six years earlier on his first tour, enough to last a lifetime. However, after three full tours, he was the newest recruit again.

Transitioning from a seasoned regular Army grunt to a fresh-out-of-training Special Operations Forces Army grunt had probably reset a whole block of his don't-mess-with-me privileges. Now, after the toughest application process outside of Delta Force and two more years of training, he was finally FMQ—fully mission qualified—for the Night Stalkers of the 160th SOAR.

Maybe Mason had a point on at least one count: the woman had distracted him. In a full vest, flightsuit, and Army boots, she still looked amazing. Just the way she walked: happy to be here, belonging-where-she-was, whole spring-her-in-step kind of thing. He guessed that alone set her outside the norm for central Iraq.

He grabbed his helmet and set off at a jog beside Mason, out of the brightly lit hangar and onto the night-shrouded tarmac toward the rescue bird.

Elsewhere across the field, other helos were roaring to life. Four Black Hawks, a massive Chinook, and a couple Little Birds. The Night Stalkers were going out in force tonight, which was so sweet for a first mission. And if everything went right, he'd be bored out of his gourd—because that's what every CSAR flight wanted to be.

Combat Search and Rescue was about going into the guts of the fight and hauling out whoever had caught the worst of it. A CSAR's ideal mission was when they circled for hours out past the five-minute hold line and never got the call.

But if the hot lady and her companion had to go in, he and Mason were there to keep them safe. Xavier liked running protection detail. He didn't mind the battle when he was in it, but he preferred the far less glorious role of rescuing the wounded. He never gave it much thought, and jogging up to his bird for the first time wasn't when a dude should start thinking.

The Black Hawk waiting for them wasn't some standard Geneva Agreement-Red Cross bearing-and-no-mounted-weapons bird. It was ten tons of pitch black nasty with a pair of side-mounted M134 Miniguns that could lay down six thousand rounds of havoc per minute.

Army, Navy, Air Force's 724th Pararescue—all those guys flew air ambulances that had to be marked clearly by international treaty and were forbidden to carry any but light personal weapons for protection only. It rankled that so many of the bad guys thought the big red cross was to make their targeting easier, but the US followed the rules in this even if many of the forces it faced didn't. Of course there was no law against a pair of fully-loaded Apaches or Cobras hovering on close guard—which was standard operating practice for most teams.

Most of the Spec Ops teams depended on the 724th Pararescue to drag out the wounded. But for the Night Stalkers, they were typically so far past the enemy's (or a supposed friendly's) line that there was no way for the Air Force to get to them in time. So, of all the spec ops outfits, only the 160th SOAR lofted their own CSAR med teams.

As the helicopter transport team for Delta Force, SEAL Team 6, and the 75th Rangers—the Night Stalkers flew under different rules by definition. They always flew into the heart of the battle, well past the lines where anyone would pay attention to whether or not it was a medical flight.

Glory hounds never made it to the Night Stalkers and Xavier was good with that. Too many from the old neighborhood cared more about their "reps" than their lives. Doofuses.

So, instead of air ambulances ready to launch at a moment's notice, SOAR sent their own well-armed warbirds —ones that just happened to carry medics. The medheads were soldiers first and wore no Red Cross armbands of supposed "protection." But they had the training and carried enough gear that they could do almost anything, including open heart surgery if necessary. The Black Hawks went in armed just to make sure they stayed safe.

"What's our op tempo?" he asked Mason as they secured their gear inside their bird.

"You like the ground?"

Xavier shrugged, not knowing what he was after.

"Better kiss it goodbye. Won't be seeing it much until you rotate back stateside."

"I don't mean the regiment. I mean us, CSAR."

For a guy who talked so much, Mason's sudden silence was eloquent.

Shit!

NOREEN WALLACE WATCHED the new guy. Hard to miss. He stood half a head taller than The Jar and a shoulder wider— he was as big as her older brother, maybe even bigger. Her brother wore his curly hair short, despite her teasing him to cut it off so that he'd look like Luther in the *Mission Impossible* movies—Ving Rhames might be old, but he was still a total stud.

This guy's head was smooth-shaved like Ving's. But trotting along in full combat gear made him look way more powerful than any mere movie star ever could.

He moved at a brisk pace and made it look easy. You didn't make it into Spec Ops without a lot of running, but he *looked* like a runner: smooth and fast despite his heavy load.

Barry started calling out the list and she turned to check the gear hanging on every inside surface of the Black Hawk's cargo bay: blood supply in the cooler, saline and antibiotics fully restocked, bandages okay in seven different sizes from cut to catastrophic. Barry read over a hundred items off the checklist and she verified every one—didn't even have to search to find them, their position was long since hardwired into her nervous system.

The Jar and the new guy were preflighting the helo. Both moved with the smooth efficiency of long practice.

He kept an eye on her, but kept his words to himself as he worked.

Within three minutes, the crew chiefs were aboard and checking their guns while the pilot and copilot started up the engines. As soon as they fed her power, she and Barry checked the heart monitors, defib, and IV infusion pumps.

New Guy finished his preparations just as she finished item #103: water bottle to stay hydrated in the parching desert that had once been northern Iraq but now was simply a disaster.

They turned toward each other at the same moment. He didn't balk or act awkwardly. Instead he held out a hand that completely enveloped hers when they shook.

"Guardian of the Night, huh? Or do you prefer Angel of Death?"

So, The Jar had already been telling him stories and he hadn't shied off. Good sign there. Though if she could think of a worse name to stick The Jar with, she'd do it. "Jar Jar Binks" maybe? Tempting, but that would be downright nasty. Not her style. She had fun teasing the Master Sergeant, but didn't want to hurt him.

"Stick with Guardian and we'll get on fine. Though you missed 'The Bitch of Black Death' and—" She shrugged. A long litany of nicknames had marked her past, like mile markers on the highway; this was only the latest.

He smiled rather than backing away. "Guessin' you kinda forced 'Guardian of the Night' down their throats."

"Got it in one."

His smile was a dazzler, and there was no doubt that he knew it. This was *not* her brother John. John was the big-hearted storyteller of any crowd with an eager laugh and a soft manner—behind which hid the Number Two mechanic in the Night Stalkers. He was the first to acknowledge that his wife, Connie, ranked Number One—whose shy smiles were so rare that Noreen sometimes teased her fair-skinned sister-in-law that it was time to start cataloging them.

"You got a name or do I just call you Guardian?"

"Lieutenant Noreen Wallace. You?"

"Staff Sergeant Xavier Jones."

She could see him wince ever so slightly, as if his name hurt him.

No, it would be the obvious nickname: The X-Man. Or Egghead. Both were bad and inevitable—and way too obvious. Professor X, Charles Xavier, the bald leader of the comic book X-Men. Xavier looked the role: massive and imposing in a way that a little white guy like Patrick Stewart only pulled off in the movies by being so smart. Sergeant Jones's power was out there for all to see.

"Nice to meet you, 'Captain Luc'." She waited while he

blinked once, twice, then tugged down on his Kevlar vest the same way Patrick Stewart always had tugged his uniform as Captain Jean-Luc Picard of Star Trek's *Enterprise.*

"Pleased to meet you, Miss Guardian," he said in his big deep voice, with all of the formality a starship captain would have used.

She laughed and he grinned back at her. You had to be more than just sharp to make it into the Night Stalkers. You had to be smart as hell. And to get a pass from her, a background in comics and science fiction was essential.

The helo lifted, and she and Barry slid the side doors of the Black Hawk's cargo bay closed. Xavier swung into his seat, snapped his vest to the safety harness, and yanked his helmet's visor down. Even behind all that gear, he still stood out for his sheer size. It was a wonder he could cram into the tight gunner's seat at all.

As with every flight, she sent a prayer to whoever was listening up there that she'd have no work tonight. A prayer that was answered far too rarely.

XAVIER SAT FACING sideways behind the pilot seat, his Minigun on an armature that reached out through the hull and offered a wide range of fire in defense of the bird.

He watched the tactical display running across the inside of his visor. The main flight was in the lead by twenty kilometers and five minutes. They were down at NOE. Nap-of-Earth flight was better than the best roller coaster at the county fair, and nobody flew the track like a Night Stalker pilot. Ten tons of helo zipped along less than fifty feet above the ground: hugging hills, slicing past trees, dodging houses.

He kept his hands firmly on his Minigun's handles, using it

and his harness for bracing. The mission briefing had said they were flying through the Zagros Mountains where they'd gotten word of a large terrorist team on the move. He'd done six half-year deployments during his previous three tours and knew this part of Northeastern Iraq too well. It was like coming home—to a nightmare, but as much of a home as he'd ever had.

"Beats the shit out of Mobile," he mumbled to himself, then heard it in the headphones built into his helmet. Open intercom.

" 'Bama boy?" the male medic asked.

"Army boy," was all Xavier was now.

"Name is Barry, if anyone cares."

"Sorry, Barry. My bad. Noreen's such a damn dazzler. Don't know how you can form a coherent sentence working alongside someone like that."

"Hey, I'm right here listening."

"Yes, ma'am." Wouldn't have been any point in teasing her if she wasn't.

"Don't I know it. I feel invisible around her," Barry had an easy sense of humor, which Xavier liked about him. "And everybody's from somewhere."

"Not me." Xavier wasn't quite sure how to bull his way out of this one—not bullshit, but rather bull in china shop to get away from the topic. "Born in the Army."

"You got a name, or do I just call you Rookie?"

"Sorry, dude. Name is Xavier Jo—"

"Captain Luc," Noreen declared. "Cap'n for short."

"Name is Cap'n Luc," Xavier tried not to miss a beat, "nice rank bump there. And I'm from nowhere. I got beamed aboard when I hit Fort Benning for Basic Training. Rest of before that…" he shuddered. Rest of before that he did his best to never think about.

The two medics sat in jump seats at the back of the cargo

bay. Funny how far away ten feet felt when his other side was rubbing against the back of the pilot's seat.

"Why Guardian of the Night?" he asked over the intercom, wondering how such a pleasant woman struck such terror into an old hand like the master sergeant.

"Angel of Death," The Jar groaned like a lost soul.

"I answer to both," Noreen happily agreed.

Xavier liked her voice, a winning combination of warmth and sass. He'd spent three months working with a British team in Baghdad during his second deployment. Cyril would have called her cheeky—it worked on her.

"Why?"

"You'll see," Mason sounded grim.

"Should have been a dwarf named Mopey for you, Mason."

The master sergeant growled, reminding Xavier exactly who outranked him here—everybody.

But Noreen's bright laugh told him it was worth the price he was bound to pay.

ABOUT THE AUTHOR

M.L. Buchman started the first of, what is now over 50 novels and as many short stories, while flying from South Korea to ride his bicycle across the Australian Outback. Part of a solo around the world trip that ultimately launched his writing career.

All three of his military romantic suspense series—The Night Stalkers, Firehawks, and Delta Force—have had a title named "Top 10 Romance of the Year" by the American Library Association's *Booklist.* NPR and Barnes & Noble have named other titles "Top 5 Romance of the Year." In 2016 he was a finalist for Romance Writers of America prestigious RITA award. He also writes: contemporary romance, thrillers, and fantasy.

Past lives include: years as a project manager, rebuilding and single-handing a fifty-foot sailboat, both flying and jumping out of airplanes, and he has designed and built two houses. He is now making his living as a full-time writer on the Oregon Coast with his beloved wife and is constantly amazed at what you can do with a degree in Geophysics. You may keep up with his writing and receive a free starter e-library by subscribing to his newsletter at: www.mlbuchman.com

Join the conversation:
www.mlbuchman.com

Other works by M. L. Buchman:

SIGN UP FOR M. L. BUCHMAN'S NEWSLETTER TODAY

and receive:
Release News
Free Short Stories
a Free Starter Library

Do it today. Do it now.
www.mlbuchman.com/newsletter

Printed in Great Britain
by Amazon